HAUNTED HONEYMOON

CONFESSIONS OF A CLOSET MEDIUM
BOOK 7

NYX HALLIWELL

Haunted Honeymoon, Confessions of a Closet Medium, Book 7

Nyx Halliwell

February 14, 2023

ISBN: 978-1-948686-84-6

Cover Art by Fanderclai Design **www.fanderclai.com**

Formatting by Beach Path Publishing, LLC

ONE

"Look at that beautiful blue sky." Logan wraps an arm around my waist and tugs me close. The motorboat slices through the Gulf waters, bobbing up and down on the waves with carefree abandon. "It will be nice to finally have you all to myself for a few days."

I've secured a wide brimmed hat to my head and I tip my face up to see the cloudless canopy over us. It's the same color as his eyes. The air smells salty, and our skipper wears the distinctive cologne of fish. He's deeply tanned and mostly grunts, rather than using words to confirm or deny our comments or requests. "Nice of the judge to offer us this retreat. Not everyone has their own private island."

Spindrift blows in our faces as the boat easily cuts through another wave. The motor revs and I grab Logan's arm to steady myself on the padded seat.

"He hasn't even been here yet. Claims he got the whole place, land and resort, for less than half the market value."

"That's what happens when a hurricane leaves behind a lot of destruction."

"But the main house is intact and fully staffed. It's the perfect getaway," he insists over the motor noise. "Nothing but sand, sun, and relaxation."

And no ghosts. The words go unspoken but I know he's thinking them.

I am, too.

Until the spirit smiling at me from the prow shoots that dream in the foot. She hovers close to the captain and wears a sundress that drips water. Her hair is stringy and caked with mud and grass.

His wife, I assume, since they wear matching bands on their left ring fingers. She must have drowned years ago, since she looks three decades his junior and the dress hasn't been in style for at least that long.

I hate to ignore her, but I'm as determined as Logan to take a break from the quirky, and sometimes downright dangerous, world of spirits. Over the past year, my life has been full of them.

Each one needs help, and I'm exhausted from the never-ending dramas they create. The threats to me and mine are enough to make me crazy, and I have constant nightmares. Admitting this is embarrassing but I've become paranoid, even in my own home.

The late afternoon sun glints off the water, creating a glimmering mirror effect. We round a bend of towering pines and the edge of the property comes into view. I sigh at the sight of the wooden dock and the peaceful scenery behind it.

Logan is right—this is exactly what we need. Long walks on the beach, a couple's massage, romantic dinners—

it's all I've been wishing for. I've brought a few novels and my sketchbook, and I can't wait to enjoy peace and quiet and let my muse inspire me.

As we near the shore, the captain cuts the motor and we coast to the dock. On closer inspection, it seems a bit rickety. I wonder if it's a trick of the light, but the thing seems to list to one side. The wood is bleached and warped. Several planks of the walkway are gone, others have chunks missing, as if the monster from the Jaws movie has used them to snack on.

The once exclusive resort suffered after the edge of a recent hurricane swiped by it a few years ago. Unable to restore it to its former glory, the then-owners abandoned the island and sold it to Judge Barlow.

According to what he's told us, a few of the original staff members who called the small island home have stayed on as his employees, managing the house and grounds, and rebuilding the structures deemed salvageable.

"Is that our welcoming party?" I squint at what appears to be a goat waiting at the end of the dock, jaws chewing on something. He's dappled gray and brown with white legs and wearing a straw hat.

"That's Fred," the ghost tells me.

Her husband just grunts, lifting a heavy coiled rope and tossing it onto the landing. We bob alongside the pier and he hops onto the wooden planks, securing a loop around a post.

Logan assists me out of the boat and a whiff of the goat makes me scrunch up my nose. Fred wears a straw hat similar to mine, yet much smaller. It's tattered along the edges, much like the dock.

Our skipper hauls our luggage to the beach where he

drops it onto the white sand. "Be back in three days," he says, with no further instructions.

"Which way to the house?" Logan calls.

The man's boots kick up sand, his retreat a hasty one. He purposely avoids the goat, still standing on the dock, watching all of us. As the man passes him, the animal fills his lungs and lets out a loud, and very grating, bleating noise.

A gust of wind swoops around us and lifts my hat off my head. It spirals out and away, landing in the water.

"Oh, no." I struggle to run in the loose sand. It's inside my sandals and I kick them off. I can hear Mama right now, telling me my fair skin will be covered with freckles in no time.

"I'll get it." Logan puts out a hand to tell me to stay put and trots down the beach to the waves that roll gently in and out. The hat floats toward him, then away. He kicks off his loafers and tugs off his socks before venturing in. "Nice and warm," he shouts.

The motorboat starts with a grinding clang and kicks up a rooster tail of water as the captain takes off with a flourish. I point to the boat growing smaller and smaller. "It's almost like he couldn't wait to leave."

"What?" Logan snags the hat, holding it up. Soggy, it folds in his hand and the breeze flings droplets onto his linen shirt.

"Nothing." I wave my comment off, scanning the shoreline. A hundred yards away is a graveyard of similar boats and partial structures that must have been damaged in the storm.

He trudges back, shoes and socks in his other hand, and holds out the wet hat.

Definitely getting freckles. I accept it and together, we reassemble ourselves before he picks up our luggage.

"There's a footpath over there." I point to the overgrown forest. This isn't exactly the start I'd envisioned, but at least there aren't any ghosts here on the beach. *Please let the woods be free of them, too.* "Is that the way to the main house?"

"Must be." The sun bathes his hair in a golden light as he gives me a rallying smile and slight bow. "I'd hoped for a porter, but looks like I'll be assisting you with your baggage today, milady."

"Such formality." I grin and lift my nose in the air, affecting the look of the rich and famous. "Carry on, then, bellhop. Take me to my room."

The way is overly shaded from the trees and vegetation that at one time must have been well cared for but now closes in around us. A loud reverberating noise echoes in my ears as an enormous mosquito dive bombs my head and ends up on my arm. I swat it away, trying not to shriek at its gigantic long legs and nasty proboscis intent on drawing my blood.

"Hope they have insect repellent," Logan says. He's starting to sweat.

I am, too, and not only because of the heat and humidity. I'm used to that, being from Georgia, but this is *tropical.* I'm more concerned about the fact all of this feels...off.

The path narrows further and I have to walk in front of him. A glance back tells me the goat has decided to accompany us, several stalks of sea grass sticking out from the side of his mouth. He chews as he ambles along, and the mosquito hitches a ride on the beast's hat.

Flat stones peek out from moss. The rambling path has several downed palm trees that Logan and I have to climb over or walk around in order to follow it. The gloom grows deeper when clouds blot out the sun and the canopy above us seems to sag lower and lower the farther in we go. The rustle of leaves and the scratching of nails suggest a variety of critters are watching us from their hiding places.

My nerves are getting to me the longer our trek becomes. Insects sing, frogs croak, and Fred continues to keep pace with us, his odor making me choke.

"I'm ready for that cocktail," Logan says as we round a mammoth rock that seems to mark the end of the trail. A sign, now lying in the sand, is faded. I can make out its former message, telling us the main house is one direction and the spa accommodations are the opposite. The only trouble is, I can't tell which way is which since it's no longer secured in the ground.

"I wonder if it's too late to ask the captain to come back," I say under my breath.

"What?"

"Nothing." I offer a bright smile that I don't feel, turning the sign with its arrows one way and then the other. "Which way, bellhop?"

Logan sets down the luggage and wipes his brow. He glances around, bends slightly and squints. "Hey, look there. Is that the mansion?"

I follow the direction he points through a clump of bushes and see the remnants of a garden. Past that, a large fountain with an enormous stone pineapple in its center that once must have produced a steady waterfall still stands. Currently, it's sporting moss instead of a gentle stream.

It's the first sign of civilization, outside of the goat and his jaunty hat, and relief sweeps through me. "Whatever it is, I hope there's a big old-fashioned bathtub for me to soak in." I hold up one foot and then the other to rid the sand from my shoes. "Let's check it out."

Once more lifting our bags, he follows. The path becomes wider, the vegetation less dense. Remnants of a lawn are present in front of a sweeping drive that arches up and away from the two-story Gothic mansion the judge told us was unharmed and still staffed.

"Finally." I trudge forward, ignoring the fact the house facade appears more like a creepy, horror film setting than a carefree island manor.

Logan joins me at the bottom of the steep staircase. Like the dock, the steps are missing chunks of stone and crumbling in other places. Gargoyles with monkey faces stare down at us from the towering roof and the upper windows are boarded over.

Wooden slats used as siding are faded and broken in spots. Even the once grand double front doors seem tired, and the bronze handles have a length of chain-link through them with a padlock.

"I think the realtor might have downplayed the extent of the storm damage," Logan says, glancing around, as if hoping for another mansion that might be the one we're looking for.

"Hello?" I call, the word echoing off the deserted house. "Anyone home?"

Fred climbs the stairs, avoiding the damaged areas, and faces us with a hair-raising bleat. The sound makes me cover my ears and step back.

"I wonder if it's too late to get a boat ride out of here,"

Logan murmurs, pacing down the sidewalk that leads around the side of the mansion.

"Oh, hello." A butler appears on the veranda and smiles at me. "Welcome to Blue Parrot Isle and Resort. How can I help you?"

I take several steps away from the staircase, nearly tripping over the luggage in my haste.

"What is it?" Logan calls. "Is something wrong?"

Lots of things about this place are wrong, but especially this man dressed in his smart butler's uniform and smiling down at me, who doesn't realize he's no longer alive.

TWO

"There's a bloody ghost, isn't there?" Logan marches back to me. He grabs his phone and punches in a number. "We're getting out of here. We'll go back to the mainland and find a nice, very expensive and lavish hotel for the weekend."

"I'm afraid the satellite was damaged in the storm," the butler says. "There's no cell service."

"You won't get through," I tell Logan reluctantly. I hate to confirm his suspicion about the ghost, but it is what it is. "Satellite's gone."

He grimaces at the screen, seeing the lack of bars, and swears loud enough the nearby palms tremble. Several chickens emerge from the bushes and begin pecking at the ground nearby. "You've got to be kidding."

"Is there any way off the island today?" I ask the ghost. Logan follows my pinpoint gaze, a semi-hopeful expression on his face. Maybe my gift will provide us with helpful information.

The butler hovers a few inches off the veranda, both

white-gloved hands making a dismissive gesture. "Heavens, no." He half peeks over his shoulder and from the corner of my eye, I catch movement behind a curtained window. When I glance that way though, the lace is moving faintly but there's no one there. The butler's face falls ever so slightly, then the corners of his mouth turn upward as he looks toward me again. "Might as well come in and make yourselves comfortable."

I give a disappointed shake of my head to Logan, who swears again, more quietly this time. He stalks off, holding his phone in the air. I know his logical and strategic mind is running through various ideas, but he's also not opposed to a miracle.

"What's your name?" I ask the butler.

He gives a grand sweep of one arm toward the entrance. "I'm Sid. Welcome to our peaceful sanctuary. How long will you be staying with us?"

Not long, hopefully. Leaving Logan to pace and mutter, I ascend the staircase, careful of the gaps in the wood and moving aside a large palm frond that blocks the top. It slaps me in the face. "Ow!"

I toss it over the steps and the roving chickens scatter.

The butler floats toward the grand entrance, looking less than grand these days. The paint is faded and the sign bolted to the wood next to it announces the Blue Parrot was originally founded in 1876. "Careful, my dear."

The odor from the goat makes me put a hand over my nose when I get to the top. "We planned to stay the weekend, but we anticipated the resort was still habitable."

"Oh, don't worry." He makes that gesture again, completely unconcerned about our dilemma. "We have a generator and plenty of delicious food. Our chef comes from a long line of indigenous folks who sure knew how to cook. He's even been featured in culinary magazines!"

Movement behind the curtained window again snags my attention. I can't make out anyone and my curiosity is peaked. "The generator still works?"

"It did until it ran out of gas. When was that?" He taps a finger to his chin. "Or maybe it didn't. I can't remember for some reason."

I hold in my sigh as I meet his gaze. "And where would we get more gas for it if it is empty?"

He gives me a stumped expression. "You'll have to ask Rommy. He's the handyman. Fixes anything that breaks. I'm not good with that stuff."

Crossing my fingers, I glance around. "Where is he?"

The goat howls and I flinch, covering my ears and taking several steps back. The butler makes shooing motions at him. "Get out of here. Go!"

Fred appears to see and hear Sid—animals are often able to interact with the dead—and slowly ambles down the stairs, still chewing on his grass. The chickens rush to him and follow him around the yard.

"He's cute," I lie. "Adds to the island ambiance."

"He's a demon from hell," the butler claims with grave menace in his tone. As if he's realized his welcoming personality has shifted, he covers his mouth for a split second, shakes his head, and his features instantly morph into a smile once more. He motions at the door. "Let's get you checked in, shall we?"

He fades through the double wooden entrance. I glance back at Logan. The chickens have already abandoned the goat and now flock around my husband's feet. "Any chance you can break this lock?"

He's still punching buttons on his phone, but the last of his hope about a miracle fades like Sid's spirit. He pockets the device reluctantly and jogs up the hole-filled steps with graceful ease. Taking my hands in his, he sighs deeply. "I'm so sorry, Ava."

In the distance, I hear a rooster crow. Palm fronds clatter in the breeze and warm air wraps around us. While the place is in need of repairs, the landscape is pretty and here in the shade of the veranda, the temperature is perfect. I squeeze his hands and give him a bolstering smile. "We'll figure it out. There's a generator and possibly a living person named Rommy. We'll find him."

Logan perks up. "The ghost told you all that?"

I nod. "His name is Sid and he doesn't seem to realize he's you-know-what."

"Of course he doesn't." Logan eyes the chain and lock, raises a leg, and kicks the double doors. Wood splinters. The lock and chain clang as they hit the threshold, and the doors bang open.

"Look at you, being all He-Man," I tease.

"Cheap lock." He studies the foyer before assisting me over the pile and through the entrance. We're welcomed by sleek teak floors and a high ceiling with an antique chandelier. "Whoa. This place was nice once."

Indeed, the interior is grand, sporting white pillars and two sweeping staircases, one on each side. There's even a tree growing up through the center of the floor, its branches reaching past the second story balcony and toward a skylight high overhead.

Chickens race in like they've found a new roost. I manage to chase a few out, but they're crafty and avoid my attempts. I close the doors behind us.

A variety of large framed paintings hang on the walls, each featuring a native plant of the island. Above every one is a spotlight and they're all on. A good sign since I assume they're powered by electricity. Maybe Rommy *has* already filled the generator's tank.

Sid stands behind a raised wooden desk on our left, studying an open registry ledger. "I'm afraid I don't see any visitors listed for arrival today." He glances up at us. "What were your names again?"

"Logan and Ava Cross. We were invited by the new owner, Judge Mitchell Barlow. We're celebrating our honeymoon."

Sid frowns. "New owner? Oh, that's not good."

"You didn't know the island had been sold?"

Logan sends me a questioning look.

"We knew it was in the works, but you see..." Sid stops himself. "Never mind." Whirling around to intently study another book behind him on a shelf under a set of skeleton keys, he nods. There is no computer here, and he can't shift through pages because of his incorporeal form. He also can't lift the key from the hook, although he tries. "Looks like you're in luck. The honeymoon suite is available. If I can just grab this key."

And here it is, my opening to explain to him that he's dead and that's why he can't. I wonder how he died and how long ago. If it's recent, which is likely, where is his body? What caused his death? He looks fit and no older than my dad. Obviously, he wasn't expecting it and that's why he's still hanging around. "We'll check out the room in a bit. Where is everyone?"

Yes, I'm avoiding tackling the D word. Some folks get angry and act out when they discover they're a ghost. I'd prefer to get more information from him before I delve into it.

"We're here," a woman's voice says, and I see three more ghosts filing out from a closed door under one of the staircases. She wears a maid uniform. "Sorry, we're weren't expecting guests today."

"What's going on?" Logan asks. He's again following my gaze as it bounces from the tall, slender maid to a chubby, fat-cheeked man wearing a chef's hat. Beside him is another man, dressed in greasy overalls and a straw hat, not much different from the goat's. "There's more than one now, isn't there?"

"All four of the staff have arrived," I explain. To them, I say, "I'm Ava and this is Logan. We came for our honeymoon, but we need to leave now. A family emergency, ah... came up." I have no idea where that came from, and why I'm not honest with them, other than to be polite. One ghost who doesn't know he's dead? Sure, I can handle that. Four? I sigh, feeling my own hope for a carefree weekend puddling at my feet. "How do we get off the island?"

"There used to be a fishing charter down at the beach," the man in the hat drawls. I fear he's the Rommy that Sid has told me about. "All the boats done sunk in the storm."

That explained the debris. "Were all of you here during the hurricane?"

Logan murmurs from the corner of his mouth. "What are they saying?"

I pat his hand to ask for patience as the chef volunteers, "We rode it out, like we have plenty of times before. Thought it would be the death of me, but who knew I'd croak thanks to the curse?"

The maid shoots him a glare and smacks at his arm. "Don't be talking that nonsense."

"Wait." I glance between all of them. "You know you're...?"

"Dead?" The chef laughs and exchanges a knowing glance with his coworkers. "Mainlanders." He shakes his head. "Course we know. Nice that you can see us." He waggles a thumb at the others. "It's been downright boring with only these folks to talk to."

"I'm not going to like this, am I?" Logan strolls over to a plush library chair near a wall of bookshelves. He waves a chicken out of it, and plops down, resigned.

A breeze rushes past me and sends goosebumps down my arms. The ghosts seem to freeze for a moment, but I don't see any other spirits. I do, however, hear a low rumble. A voice? Whatever it says is lost on me, but they seem to understand it.

The maid makes a face and her voice takes on a pleading note. "Please don't leave. We've been so lonely."

I'm loathe to mention a curse to Logan, who knows firsthand how dangerous those can be. "What are your names?"

Her face brightens. "I'm Irma, this is Bernie"—she nudges the chef—"and that's...where did he go?" Overalls has disappeared. Sid joins the lineup. "You've already met Sid."

"How did you all die, if not from the storm?"

Sid crosses his white-gloved hands. "We're not quite sure."

Irma nods. "Mysterious circumstances."

Bernie snorts. "Mysterious, all right. As in, *the curse.*

There's a murderer on the loose on the island and he's done picked us off one by one."

I can't stop myself from glancing at Logan.

"What?" he demands, coming out of the chair.

As I start to answer, the entry doors fly open and bang against the walls. Pictures rattle and I whirl to find Fred on the threshold. His nerve-grating bleat, along with his suffocating barnyard smell, fills the foyer, making everyone—even the ghosts—recoil.

A goat, a curse, and ghosts. My honeymoon is off to a fantastic start.

THREE

The front doors reverberate from being slammed open, and one of the paintings on the wall now swings off-kilter.

"Did the wind do that?" Logan scans the area. "Please tell me it was wind and not another ghost."

"Fred is not the wind but he is very much alive." I make shooing motions at the goat, but he refuses to budge. In fact, he takes offense at my waving hands and charges. I swing a heavy door to block him and he shifts sideways, still managing to headbutt me in the hip.

The jarring hit sends me sprawling onto the hardwood floor.

"Ava!" Logan reaches for me, just as a tall woman steps into the entry and caresses the goat's neck.

Her lilac skirt billows around her sandy bare feet and her hair is wrapped in colorful fabric. Gold hoops big enough I could wear them as bracelets hang from each earlobe and she has a black patch over her right eye. "Fred is magical. He does not, however, control the wind."

Her voice sends a shiver through me. Logan assists me to my feet and murmurs, "She's real, right? I can see her."

Ghosts aren't *not* real, just invisible to most folks. Since I've died and come back to life, my wiring is now a bit different. I've always had "the gift" as Mama and my Aunt Willa claimed, but it's stronger after my near death event. "She is," I tell him, wiping dirt off the hem of my sundress. My sandal is askew and I twist my foot to right it. "Persephone would love her."

The woman narrows her eyes at a spot over my shoulder. "You don't belong here. Leave."

Glancing back, I watch as the ghosts disappear. I face her again. "You can see them?"

She sniffs with disdain. Yep, my guardian angel would be thoroughly delighted with this gal. "You must leave, too. *Now*."

Interesting that she doesn't seem to care I can also see spirits. "Tell us how and we will."

"You shouldn't have come in the first place."

Is she possibly the one who killed the staff? Is that why they're afraid of her? *Persephone*, I call telepathically. *Need help*!

Fixing our new visitor with a charming smile, I pretend I'm not suspicious, and a little scared, of her. "The boat that brought us won't be back until Monday. We're told there is no satellite, so we can't call and request sooner transportation."

Her one visible eye blinks. "Swim."

"You're helpful," Logan says with no small amount of sarcasm.

Killer or not, this gal is rude. I don't like how she treated the ghosts, and I have the feeling I need them to return so I can ask them about her. "What's your name? Why are you here?"

"This is my home." Her chin rises and she points at her chest with a ringed thumb. "My ancestors have lived here for hundreds of years and we never left, even when the invaders came and stole the land from us for this resort." The goat bleats again, softer this time, and she continues to stroke his neck. Her bracelets jangle and the rings she wears on every finger clink with the action. "Fred says you're idiots, but harmless. It appears you're stuck here until Buku returns."

Logan frowns at me. "Fred says?"

I study the goat and ask her, "You understand him?"

Her eye glares at me. "We have a psychic connection."

Logan snorts. "I bet you do."

My experience with psychics is a mixed bag, and since I communicate with my dead many-times great grandmother when she's in cat form, I don't dismiss the idea this gal might be able to do the same with her pet.

Persephone, where are you? I'd given her strict orders not to bother us on our honeymoon. Of course, now I need her. She holds a mean grudge when provoked and seems to be purposely ignoring me. "He sorely needs a bath," I tell the woman.

"Be careful," she replies, and I'm unsure if the warning is because the goat might take offense, or she's threatening me. "Leave this island."

Logan shifts slightly in front of me, my protector. "Careful of what?"

She peeks over each of her shoulders as if someone might be behind her—one of the ghosts, perhaps?—then lowers her voice to barely above a whisper. "Beware of the curse. It is nothing to mess with."

It's official—our honeymoon has turned into a nightmare. No amount of sunshine and tropical breezes will fix this.

Logan throws his hands up. "A curse. Great." He rolls his eyes. "Look, we came here for a little R and R. That's it. Not to talk to ghosts or break any kind of curse, hex, or evil eye hoodoo-voodoo stuff. We're going to find a room to sleep in, some food to eat, and we'll be out of here come Monday." He puts an arm around my shoulder. "You all need to leave us alone in the meantime."

I admire his perseverance and resolve. I still feel an obligation to help the staff and make sure this woman isn't the one who did them in. "What happened to the employees?"

Her eye glints oddly in the light. "Murdered." The goat lifts his muzzle and brays like a donkey, the sound hitting the high ceiling and grating down my spine like sharp nails raking my vertebrae. She pats his head as the racket dies away. "And Fred predicts you're next."

FOUR

Logan's arm tightens around my shoulders. "Murdered? By who? You?"

My husband isn't one to beat around the bush. It's the lawyer in him. He's good at cross-examination and getting confessions out of people.

If she *is* the perpetrator, however, it might be wise to not confront her without a weapon in hand. She doesn't look dangerous, but I've encountered plenty of folks—both dead and alive—who've fooled me with their intentions and level of homicidal tendencies. "Ah, sweetie," I say in my most congenial tone, tugging on Logan's arm, "don't be silly. Ms...., um, what did you say your name was?"

"I didn't." She tosses her colorful head. "You may call me Wasmee, and no, I didn't hurt anyone." She eyes Logan with speculation. "What do you know about curses, hexes, and voodoo, boy?"

He doesn't show his annoyance at the term, but I feel him tense. "My question first—who murdered the staff? Does it have to do with this curse?"

"You don't get to order me around. This island belongs to me. You have no—"

"This island does not, in fact, belong to you. It belongs to my friend. Now,"—he plants his feet and subtly edges me behind him, "answer my questions, or I'll find a way to truss you up until the boat arrives Monday, at which point, I'll haul your psychic a—"

I pinch him. "Logan!"

He takes a deep breath and reins in his temper. "I'll drag you to the mainland and throw you in jail for trespassing, and any other charge I can figure out between now and then."

Wasmee doesn't appear the least bit worried, although she does take a step back at his intensity. "Your laws don't concern me, nor do they apply to me. We have our own law here."

He's as stubborn and relentless as she is and enunciates each of his next words. "Who. Murdered. The. Staff?"

I telepathically call to Persephone again. She wanted to tag along and bring her boyfriend, a ghost who believes he's the fictional Sherlock Holmes, but I insisted they stay in Georgia and give Logan and I some privacy. It seemed a good idea at the time, and I was dead-set—pun intended—on not needing her, because I wasn't going to engage any spirits. None. I promised myself. Now, I'm in a pickle. *Please,* I say to her. *I'm sorry I told you to stay home—I need you.*

Nada. Since she's an angel/spirit guide, she should be able to find me, no matter where I am. Yet, here I stand, no angel in sight and a potential killer running around.

I take a fortifying breath. "Tell us about the curse."

Logan throws a frown over his shoulder at me.

I shrug. "We need to know who else is here and how dangerous they might be."

Wasmee shifts ever so slightly. "The two are inter-twined. Yarwen is the son of one of the families who arrived from the north a hundred and fifty years ago. Legend says they wanted to hide from those in their home country who prosecuted them so my ancestors took them in and helped them. Then they turned on us, except for him. He was a true brother to our king, and he tried to stop the slaughter and subjugation of my people. He haunts the island and those who disrespect it. It is his curse that will walk with you every step you take. He will be everywhere you go, in your dreams, and even if you succeed in leaving Monday, you'll never escape the legend. Or him."

"Sounds like a great guy," I say under my breath. "We aren't here to disrespect you or your family home. We would, in fact, leave this instant, if we could."

Logan makes an unconvinced noise. "You're saying a dead man killed the others and will haunt us, too. Seems convenient to blame a legend that's unprovable. Who else is here besides you? Who are you working with?"

A crease appears between her brow. "Working with?"

"Scaring off investors so you and your accomplice can have the island to yourselves—nice try. What's the endgame? You plan to open your own resort? Or turn around and sell the island for a nice profit in a few years?"

The crease deepens. "You're delusional."

He points to himself. "*I'm* delusional?"

The doors blow open again and the goat walks out. Wasmee watches him go, but the way she glances at the yard beyond tells me she's ready to flee.

"Weren't the staff locals like you?" I ask. If I can keep

her talking about herself and the island, maybe I can discover something useful. "Why would Yarwen harm them?"

"Traitors," she hisses. Her earrings brush her shoulders as she glances back at me. "They worked for those who used our homeland for financial gain."

She's out the door before I can inhale and ask another question. I start to follow her and Logan grabs my hand. I call after her anyway. "Wait!"

"Let her go," he says. "I have the feeling she'll be back."

Breaking free of his grip, I rush to the exit. She and the goat are gone.

I scan the landscape, searching for any sign of her bright clothes or the rustling of the bushes to indicate which direction they went.

Logan captures my hand once more and leads me across the foyer and deeper into the house. "Come on."

"Where are we going?"

"The kitchen to start."

"For knives?"

He glances at me with a raised brow. "For sage, candles, and any other curse-breaking items we can find."

"Oh." He may not believe Wasmee, but he's wise enough not to dismiss the curse. "Good plan."

He peeks into a dark room, moves on, and I follow. "But yes, a weapon or two would also be smart."

The library is filled with floor-to-ceiling shelves, ornate furniture, and a grand piano. Every surface is covered with odds and ends, including sepia-toned photographs and antique lamps. "You've been hanging around me and my witchy friends too long."

He smiles, but it's a gloomy one. We find a massive

formal dining room, white sheets draped over the table and chairs. "I've learned to cover all my bases."

Just as we reach the kitchen at the rear of the mansion, the cook, Bernie, appears. "You shouldn't go in there," he says with a warning edge to his voice.

I stop Logan and relate that the ghost is there and what he's said.

"Why not?" I ask him.

He wrings his hands and straightens his already straight white hat. "Because."

Logan and I share a glance. "What is it?" he asks.

"Not sure. Bernie is warning me not to go in."

"Is the killer in there?" Logan asks to the invisible-to-him spirit.

Bernie shakes his head and I do the same at Logan.

"Then we're going in," he announces.

Together, we peer into the commercial kitchen, late evening sun shining through a bay window and spotlighting a long prep countertop. The smell of decay and death hit us and we both grimace and pull back, covering our noses.

With another shared look, we fortify ourselves and creep through the door, wary. A body lies face down on the floor in front of the counter.

At least a dozen knives stick out from Bernie's back. His once white hat is now crimson with blood and smashed into the tiles next to him.

"Poor Bernie," I say, and the ghost gives me a sad nod.

Logan examines the corpse, pointing to the excess amount of knives. "It appears our killer has anger issues."

Bernie waves at the countertop. A box of elbow macaroni and a cutting board with moldy cheese rests on it.

"Please don't reveal that macaroni and cheese was my last meal." He meets my eyes, a bit abashed. "It was my favorite comfort food, you see. There were no guests and I needed to cook—the stress of the storm and all had gotten to me. But a world-renown chef should have a finer palate. If this gets out...it could ruin my reputation."

Pretty sure that's not our biggest problem at the moment. "Being raised in the South, I completely understand," I reassure him. "It's my opinion that mac-n-cheese could do a lot to make the world a better place."

Logan glances at me, curiosity curving the corner of his mouth. "Amen to that."

Relief softens Bernie's features. "Thank you. I couldn't agree more."

Keeping that secret is easy. Finding our angry killer, not so much.

FIVE

"This is a crime scene," Logan announces, holding out an arm to block me from getting closer. "Since there doesn't seem to be law enforcement on the premises, I'll take photos and videos, then move him into the cooler to preserve the body."

Across the way is an enormous walk-in refrigerator and freezer combo. Our blurry selves reflect in the stainless steel doors marred with specks of dried blood. "If he was stabbed here,"—I point to Bernie on the floor—"how did blood get over there?"

Logan is quiet for a long moment, probably recreating the scene in his head. I'm doing the same. We scan the floor, the cabinets, the assorted other appliances, and a hanging rack of pots and pans.

"It appears the initial attack took place near the refrigeration unit," Logan says. "He stumbled to the counter and fell to the ground." He steps closer to peer at the macabre scene and directs my attention to the knives below the uppermost one buried between the shoulder blades. "These lower wounds may have been postmortem. It's hard to tell, but the majority of the blood appears to have come from this one. See how it ran in this direction? The lower wounds are nearly blood-free."

My stomach gives a lurch and I swallow hard, looking away and trying to calm my nerves.

A glance at Bernie's spirit confirms my husband's summary when he nods. "Whoever got me did a bang up job," he says softly. "With my own knives, even. Who would do such a thing?"

"You don't know who it was?" I ask.

He shakes his head. "I saw a reflection, a blur, when I went to get the milk out of the cooler." The ghost puts his hands up in a *I don't know* gesture as Logan watches me, waiting for me to fill him in.

I do before continuing to quiz Bernie. "You said you saw a reflection." I glance at the refrigerator. "Was the person taller than you? The angle of the weapon in your upper back suggests they were."

He frowns in concentration. "All I remember is seeing movement, probably an arm rising and falling. It all happened so fast."

I depict what occurred for Logan and he seems thoughtful. "Ask him if he heard anything—did the killer make any noises? Say anything? Did his or her shoes make a noise? When he was first struck and stumbled to the counter, did he notice anything else that might help us figure out who did this?"

Bernie stares at his bloodied hat on the floor. "I heard whistling right before it happened. I'm not sure if that was the killer or someone else."

I wish I could make this easier for him. "You were the first who was attacked, I take it?"

He shrugs. "I guess. I wasn't sure what was going on—didn't realize I was dead. I tried talking to Irma, Rommy, and Sid, but they couldn't hear me. I could float through walls and do flips in the air." This actually brings a smile to his face. It dissolves quickly, though.

"Did you remember ever hearing Irma, Rommy, or Sid whistle?"

"Doesn't everyone on occasion? I've heard humming when the windows were open, but not whistling. It came from the garden. I never knew who it was but it was... haunting. Sad."

"Could you tell if it was a man or a woman?"

"If I had to guess, I'd say a woman."

I recount what he's told me to Logan, who nods. "Could it be Wasmee?"

"She's a spitfire, that one." Bernie chuckles. "My mother and hers grew up together, and I knew her in school, but most of us stayed away from her. She's always been a bit"—he makes a motion with his finger to suggest she's crazy—"different, but she's not a murderer."

"How can you be sure?" I ask.

He glances toward the window. "She wants the island to revert back to the way it was, but she also wants it to be a sanctuary for our people. For the plants and the birds, and everything else. Why would she kill me when I'm as much of a native as she is?"

Once again, I bring Logan up to speed. When I'm finished, Bernie has disappeared. I share that as well before I ask, "Where do you think the other bodies are?"

Logan places his hands on his hips. "I have the feeling

we're going to find out. We need one of the furniture covers from the library."

I offer to retrieve it, but he insists on going with me. Can't take any chances if a killer is still around.

The dust on the huge cloth makes me sneeze as we shake it out and return to the kitchen. Logan goes about documenting the room and the body and instructs me to stand back while he shifts Bernie onto the sheet. Feeling helpless, I join in anyway. We're as careful as we can be, and the refrigeration unit is cool inside. "The generator is definitely running," I say. "Sid thought it might be out of gas."

"Hope it doesn't quit any time soon." Logan covers the corpse with the edge of the sheet after we position the chef in the rear of the cooler. "Or this guy will smell even worse."

I wipe my forehead and snag a bottle of iced tea from a wire shelf. I'm parched and feeling lightheaded.

Logan notices several salads and miniature sandwiches nearby. "I'm starving."

"You can eat at a time like this?"

He gives me a sly grin. "I can always eat."

Collecting a meat tenderizer and a wicked looking serrated knife as weapons, we take the food to a settee on the back porch, the low sun casting long shadows over the gardens. I feel awkward eating, but I'm famished, and the sandwiches are delicious. Bernie has added watercress and avocado to the chicken and cheese creations. Cramming our stomachs full, I hope it's not the last meal Logan and I enjoy together.

"Do you like the dressing?" Bernie pops in, smiling as I

swallow a bite of salad. "It's my secret sauce, but I'll tell you this much—fresh dill makes all the difference."

I chew and dab at the corner of my mouth with a cloth napkin that has the resort's logo embroidered on it. "Delicious."

"I made those for the staff, but obviously..." he trails off, then shakes himself. "I'm glad my final creations aren't going to waste. A chef is an artist, you know." He raises his chin proudly. "I'm a connoisseur of all the island's fruits, vegetables, and herbs. Fish, chicken, duck—we have a lot of fowl here—I know the most mouthwatering ways to prepare all of it." His face falls. "But now..."

He winks out, as if he can't stand to think about the fact he won't be cooking any longer.

Logan and I finish in silence, then he stands, tossing his napkin on the table and holding out a hand to me. Break time is over. "Let's locate the others," he says.

Reluctantly, I slip my fingers into his and rise as well. We grab our weapons. "I hope we discover a wine cellar before we come across the next body."

He quirks a brow and the corner of his mouth turns up again. "Really?"

"Don't judge." I let his censuring look roll off my shoulders. "I have the feeling I'm going to need alcohol to get through this weekend."

He gently bumps his shoulder into mine as we head back inside. "I know you don't have Persephone or Sage to help with the ghost stuff, but you've got me."

I stop him on the threshold. "I'm a lucky girl," I say, and kiss him.

A braying noise that could only be our least favorite

goat echoes from overhead. We glance up, as if we can see through the ceiling to the second floor.

"How did he get up there?" Logan asks, but I swear it's said with a dose of *I don't really want to know.*

My hand once more secure in his, I lead us to the foyer and the dueling staircases. "I think the real question is, who let him in?"

"Wasmee," Logan murmurs as we climb the wide wooden treads.

"Yep, and I still need to gather supplies for breaking the curse—if there is one."

"Let's see what the goat is doing first."

The second floor is a series of bedrooms on each side of a hallway. There is a sitting area at each end.

We discover Fred in the last room we check, standing over the body of the maid.

SIX

L inens are scattered around the floor. Irma is on her back with a pale blue sheet wound around one arm and a corner of it over her face.

Logan advances slowly, surveying the space and waving his hands at the goat. Fred refuses to move at first, then relents, shuffling off to the side.

Wasmee is nowhere to be seen. Also absent: visible blood and no obvious weapon.

Logan eyes the sheet. "Did our perpetrator hit her on the head? Suffocate her?" He uses the edge of his shirt to tug the fabric away, trying not to destroy any fingerprints or other evidence the killer might have left behind.

We both flinch at the sight—her skin is mottled and gray, and her tongue sticks out. A second sheet is twisted and wrapped several times around her throat.

"Strangulation," I murmur, my heart sinking.

"Seems so." Logan replaces the cloth over her. "We can't use these linens to move her. We're going to need another furniture cover."

In the library, I gather three of the large covers, instead of one, and hand the stack to him. "Looks like we're going to need them," I say, feeling more depressed than scared.

Returning to the room, we discover the goat is gone. His odor, however, lingers. Where he stood, we notice traces of mud and sand.

I squat to look more closely and pick up another scent I can't quite place it. I motion to the mud and sand. "Do you think the goat brought this in?"

"He's pretty dirty. If I were a betting man, I'd be all in."

Logan repeats what he did in the kitchen, taking copious photos, a video, and describing the scene in great detail into a recording app on his phone. Once he's satisfied, we place Irma on our makeshift carrier and Logan carries her downstairs to the cooler.

"Irma," I call, once we've left the kitchen. The sun has gone down and Logan checks the wall switches to find which sconces are electric. Only two come on. "Can we talk?"

She doesn't respond.

"Let's see if there are candles," he says.

I follow him from room to room, searching for some. We look in drawers, cabinets, and storage bins. Nothing. An armoire has been toppled over on its side and I notice a faint outline in the palm tree wall paper. "Why do you think this is?" I ask, running my hand over the raised edges.

Logan shrugs, digging through a huge desk across the room. "In a place like this? Who knows? Maybe there's a secret wall or room behind it."

My fingernail catches on a torn section of wallpaper. I gently peel a section away and my pulse quickens. "By George, I think you're right."

Logan joins me as I use my fingers to trace a seam in the wall. My hand bumps into cool metal, and there it is—a latch.

I twist it but it's stuck.

"Let me try," Logan says.

"Please, He-Man, go for it."

He rolls his eyes but has the square door open in no time.

Behind it, we find family photo albums, the diary of a woman named Honoree, and a few dozen full whiskey bottles.

"These may be worth thousands of dollars," my husband says with a slight reverence in his voice as he holds one up to the barely there light from the hall.

I take the diary and several of the photo albums, carrying them with me.

"What do you want those for?" he asks.

"Light reading before bed, what else?"

He grins and sticks a bottle of the whiskey under his arm. "Here." Returning to the desk, he rummages in a drawer and it squeaks when he manages to yank it out farther. He grins and holds up his treasure. "I've got three candles."

"How about matches?"

His face falls and he hands the tapers to me before he searches again. Eventually, he straightens. "None."

"Back to the kitchen." I lead the way. "There has to be some."

"I'm surprised there are no hidden guns around here. Seems like the owners stashed about everything else."

"Maybe there were, but they've been taken." We exchange a glance, considering that our killer may have a new collection of them. "Knives were used on the chef and a bedsheet on the maid. Is our murderer sending a message?"

Logan nods. "It's an interesting choice of weapons, but what exactly is he trying to say? Death by vocation?"

"It means something." I glance out the window over the kitchen sink. The patio is dark; the gardens beyond nearly invisible. Clouds block out the stars. My head is starting to pound, and I'm once more wishing we'd located a wine cellar. I'm not much of a whiskey drinker. "It's starting to rain."

Thunder erupts over the sea, a flash of lightning emphasizing the storm rolling in.

"We need better weapons," Logan says.

As the shimmer of light disappears, I notice a potting shed and greenhouse in the distance. "What do you bet Rommy is out there?" I point toward the gardens. "He probably had plenty of tools and landscape equipment."

Logan nods. "Forget candles. We need flashlights."

"There are several in the mudroom," Irma says from the corner. She seems fainter than before. "Thank you for respecting my body."

"Irma's here," I tell Logan. To her, I ask, "Do you know who killed you?"

She shakes her head. "The buzzard snuck up behind me. I didn't see his face."

"You believe it was a man."

A solemn nod. "He was strong. I fought his grip, but I couldn't break it. It was like..." She pauses and sheds a tear. Hastily wiping it away, she stares at her arms and shivers. "Like he had dozens of hands. It felt like they were all over me."

"We should bag her hands," I tell Logan. "There was a struggle. She might have the killer's DNA under her nails."

She seems forlorn. "I don't understand why anyone would want me dead. I'm just a maid. My mother was before me, and her mother before her. We worked in the house and lived on our tiny farm. Never hurt no one."

I think back to the room. "Did you notice any strange smell before or during the attack?"

She frowns. "There was something. Faint, but out of place. Not soap or alcohol, but something... Sorry." She shakes her head. "I can't place it."

"Sounds like the scent was there before the goat," I say to Logan. "The killer may have deposited it without realizing it." I address Irma again. "Did you hear anyone whistling or humming before it occurred?"

"I thought I heard a whistle, faint-like. Figured it was a tea kettle downstairs. Why?"

"Not sure. Bernie mentioned hearing whistling. Do you recall anyone around here having that habit?"

"Part of the legend about Yarwen says his mother went mad after he fought with his father over their family claim and left to live with our people. She apparently hummed herself to sleep each night and left a candle burning in the front window, hoping it would guide him home."

My heart gives a little ping of sadness. "You believe this legend?"

She gives a meek smile. "Without the stories, who are we?"

"And the curse—you believe in that, too?"

"Like so many tales, it feels safer to believe than not to."

Hmm. "Did you ever hear about a way to break this curse?"

"Until Yarwen is appeased, it cannot be broken. Since he's long gone, I'm not sure how he could reconcile with anyone now."

I learned when I returned home to Thornhollow last year, that where there's a spirit, there's a way. "He needs to be reunited with his family."

Logan's attention slides back and forth between me and the spot where I'm staring at Irma.

"Quite impossible to do with all of them being dead, right?" she asks.

Not when you're a ghost whisperer. "His spirit needs to cross to the afterlife."

"How are you going to get him to do that?"

"I have my ways, but do you really believe a ghost with extra hands killed you?"

Even earthbound spirits retain a level of rational, logical thought. She makes a face as she realizes how ludicrous it sounds, but shrugs. "Who else could it be?"

Who else indeed? "Besides Wasmee, is there anyone else here who is alive?"

"Sure, there are a few misfits that live off the land. And all kinds of animals, like Fred."

"I doubt her goat strangled you."

"He doesn't belong to her. They claim he was Yarwen's."

This Yarwen fellow is growing more interesting with every tale. "And you all think the goat has been around for a hundred plus years?"

"He's been spotted every time newcomers take over the

island. They claim he's a sign that Yarwen is upset. When you see or hear him, it's time to hide."

Probably because he smells atrocious, not because he's an omen of death. "Is there anything else you can tell us that might help solve this mystery? What about these misfits?"

"None of them come near the resort. Never have. What mystery?" She seems truly confused. "Yarwen has taken out his wrath on us, and now we're ghosts."

"Why would he do that?" Wasmee's words about traitors rings in my ears. "Why would he be upset with you?"

She wrings her hands, obviously flustered. "Sid is calling. I have to go."

With that she disappears, and I throw my hands up in frustration.

"Super helpful, wasn't she?" Logan chuckles at the face I make. "There's something about all of this that doesn't add up."

"You're telling me." I stare up at the ceiling and call, "Persephone! Sherlock! Tabitha! Will someone *please* answer me?"

Nothing. I chew on my bottom lip and Logan pats my back. "Maybe they can't hear you."

"Or they're ignoring me because I told them they couldn't come with us."

He takes my hand and leads me downstairs to the mudroom. It's still raining, and a thorough search of the baskets and cabinets turns up a single flashlight with nearly dead batteries. The weak beam barely cuts through the outside gloom as we step onto the back patio.

I pull out my phone and use the flashlight app. It's

stronger, and, together, our lights reflect off a wet stone path winding through the storm-damaged estate grounds.

"Ready?" Logan asks, the flashlight in one hand and the meat tenderizer in the other.

I suck in a humid breath. "Ready," I say, even though I'm anything but.

We are soaked by the time we reach the shed and workshop, filled with equipment and tools. Our noses are assaulted by various odors of fertilizer and weed killer, but none, thankfully, from a decaying body.

I study a row of garden shears and clippers in a jumbled pile near a workbench. "Rommy must have been offed somewhere else."

Logan sorts through them, picking out a short handled sickle and testing its weight. "Can you call his ghost and ask?"

He hands me a machete and I jump when a crack of thunder makes the windows rattle. "Let's return to the house." I feel like the stupid heroine in a horror film who's about to be stabbed in the back. "If he's not in the mansion, he'll have to wait until tomorrow for us to locate his body."

We race through the pouring rain as the storm intensifies and I am chilled to the bone by the time we find towels in the downstairs bathroom to dry off.

"We need to get out of these wet clothes," Logan says. "I'll build a fire in the library hearth."

I haven't even managed to change my shirt when the generator runs out of gas for real and we are plunged into darkness.

"Great." Logan strips off his shirt and tosses it onto the floor. The fire is going and light from the flames flickers over his chest. I take a moment to admire his sculpted abs and defined biceps. "How is it we're always getting caught in some haunted building when the electricity goes out?"

Recently, we were at the Nottingham Hotel when we experienced a similar situation. I now wish we'd gone there instead. Logan forgets his shirt for a moment and kisses me. "Not exactly how we planned our first night away, is it?"

"Not even close." We finish changing and I work on drying my hair with the last clean towel. As I wrap the thick cotton around my head, I catch movement out of the corner of my eye. "Rommy? Sid?"

Persephone appears behind the oak desk. "Do I look like a man, or are you just being mean?"

I'm so filled with relief, I ignore the comment. "I could hug you right now."

"Well, that's certainly an improvement over what you typically want to do to me."

"Where have you been?"

Logan looks confused, then realization dawns. "Persephone?"

Next to the spirit guide's feet, a tabby cat appears and I laugh. "We've got backup," I tell him, then I motion the two newcomers over to the flickering flames in the hearth and tell them our story.

SEVEN

"The one in overalls is Rommy." Persephone runs a finger over a candlestick on the mantle and examines it. She's wearing an island print dress in vibrant colors with parrots all over it. "But the one you need to speak to is Hartwell, the groundskeeper."

"Hartwell? Why has no one mentioned him? Is he a ghost?"

Tabby circles my ankle before sitting on the wool rug to clean her paws. Logan can see her and she's worked a spell so he can see and hear my spirit guide as well.

Persephone, bored with the candlestick, leaves it in order to check out a bronze lamp base in the shape of a tree. "Nope."

"He's alive? Is that good or bad?"

"Could be both," she says. "Kind of depends. This estate is amazing. Did you see the artwork in the gallery on the third floor?"

"You've been on the third floor?"

"I had to check the entire place out." She says this as

if it's obvious and I haven't been begging for her help. "You know I can't come right out and tell you who the killer is."

That's the thing about spirit guides—they can give you nudges, but free will is universal law and they cannot prompt or force you to make decisions. An offshoot of that is the fact they cannot tell you certain types of information that will sway your decision making process either. It drives me batty.

Logan sits in an upholstered chair, staring at Persephone's wild dress. "If Hartwell is the killer, how can that be a good thing?"

A shoulder lifts and drops. Bored again, she floats past me and assumes a seat at the desk. "Perhaps you can capture him and bring him to justice." She smiles at my husband. "Isn't that what attorneys do?"

He leans forward in the seat, glaring at her. "I'm not law enforcement and I don't make a habit of pursuing murderers without them."

She lifts both hands, palms up. "It seems you may not have a choice."

Debating the issue isn't getting us anywhere. "Where do we find him? Does he have any guns?"

My father was once a police officer. I have a healthy respect for all kinds of weapons, but especially those. While helping many earthbound spirits to cross over, I've also encountered my share of criminals. I've grown exceptionally tired of staring down the barrel of a gun.

"You were pretty warm at the barn," is all she'll say about his location. "As far as the second question, I have no idea, and that's the truth."

Logan and I exchange a glance. "Why is he killing

these people and making a statement with the way he does it?"

She glances around and appears to rock back in the chair, even though she is as ethereal as the ghosts. "Seems rather vengeful, don't you think?"

Which reminds me, we haven't found Sid's body yet, or discovered how he was killed. My best guess is he's still in the house. I'm loathe to leave the warm library and the comfort of the fire, but I can't rest with all this going on.

My body is exhausted and my eyelids are heavy. The single thought about a killer on the loose keeps me from searching out a comfortable bed and giving in to sleep.

"We have more bodies to find, and now, Hartwell. Whether or not he's the killer, we need to talk to all of them and see what they know."

Wearily, Logan pushes himself out of the chair. "Do you want to try Sid first? Maybe he knows where his body is. You could also ask him about the whistling and humming, and that weird smell."

Tabby perks up and sniffs the air. All I can smell is wood smoke from the fire, but I wonder if her cat nose is more attuned to more subtle odors.

"Come upstairs to the bedroom where we found Irma." I motion to her and Persephone. "Maybe Tabitha can tell us what scent is in the room where she died."

We make it to the hallway when the front doors open and Fred once more crosses the threshold. He's soaked and dripping water everywhere.

Sid flickers in, chastises the goat, and disappears as lightning flashes outside.

"Those doors were secured." Logan points to Sid's receptionist desk that he'd shoved against them. The storm rages just beyond the front steps. It's much too heavy for a goat to move. "How does he keep getting in here?"

Skirting the animal who's stench has been made worse by the rain, I glance out, searching for Wasmee. Where is she riding out the storm? Is she letting the goat in? Is she trying to scare us?

I see no sign of her, but she could be hiding in the bushes or somewhere close by, invisible in the shadows. I close the doors and Logan pinches the goat's hindquarters to make him move before he scoots the heavy desk back in place. When I turn around, I see Irma rushing down the hallway carrying a mop.

"I'll get that cleaned up," she says, and then she flickers in and out like Sid.

Poof, she's gone. Tabby sniffs the air and backs away from the goat, hissing.

"I know, right?" I pinch my nose as I join her. "On top of everything else, this guy keeps showing up, and I'm beginning to wonder if his intense reek is due to the fact he's actually dead."

The goat cries and Persephone laughs. "Oh, he's alive." She glances toward the spot where Irma was. "The storm's surges are messing with their bioelectricity. You really need to cross them over, Ava."

"Not until I know who killed them." I point to the second floor. "follow me."

In the room where we found the maid, I lead Tabby to the dried mud. "Smell anything odd?"

My grandmother sniffs at the crumbled debris, then sits back on her haunches. Her orange fur ripples and I lunge for the bedspread as a flash of light illuminates the room.

Whenever she shifts from feline to human, she's devoid of clothes. Although she's perfectly happy to run around in the nude, I'm weirded out by it.

Logan politely looks away as I throw the spread across her shoulders and cover her. She gives me the side-eye, but accepts the offering with grace. She's over two hundred years old, although she doesn't look a day past forty, and she hails from Scotland. Her brogue is still quite heavy. "Ye have yourselves in quite the pickle, don't ye?"

"Monday can't come soon enough," I say. "So what do you think? Any idea what's mixed in with that mud?"

"Looks like a generous portion of sand," Persephone comments.

"Besides that. Can you tell me what that smell is?"

Tabitha leans over it as I shine the flashlight onto the floor. "Smells like dead fish."

"It's an island. Most things stink like that."

"'Tis true, and yet, there be more. Reminds me of boats and motors. Not like in my day, but in yours."

Logan sidles up to me. "Like marine gas for an engine?"

"Aye." She nods and her hair falls gently across her shoulders. "I suppose plenty of things on an island smell of such as well."

"True, but..." Logan rubs his chin and thought. "Perhaps Rommy, or whoever our killer is, has been hanging around the charter boats."

Persephone attempts to look bored again. "He might even have captained one."

"He's the handyman." I glance at Logan. "I bet he was a boat mechanic as well."

There's a crash downstairs and we all turn toward the

door. "It's probably just the goat," Logan says, raising his sickle. "But get behind me, just in case."

I do, and Tabitha falls in with us, Persephone bringing up the rear. Our conga line moves slowly down the stairs to the main floor, all of us keeping an eye peeled for any moving shadows. The flashlight's batteries finally give out, leaving us with only my cell to light the way.

We stop several times, listening closely, but can't make out any other noise outside of the storm. My nerves are frayed by the time we reach the bottom.

Logan must sense my fear and guides me inside the library. Once we are all behind the door, he shoves a chair against the doorknob to jam it. "Until the storm is over, we're staying in here."

Tabitha takes a seat near the crackling fire and Persephone begins surveying the bookshelves.

"Would you look at this?" She points to a thick volume. "It's a history of the island. Maybe there's something about this curse in it."

The way she looks at me, I know she's trying to be helpful. I take the book and add it to the stack I gathered earlier with the diary. "Any clue as to who Honoree might be?"

She points at the history book. "I bet you can find out."

And so, by the light of the fire, I start reading. Scanning chapter after chapter, I stumble across a single mention of Yarwen. At the ripe age of sixteen, he was disowned by his father, the first white settler on the island, and went to live with his mother's people. "Yarwen's mom was a native." I glance up at the others. Wasmee left that little fact out. "It says here that he began to sabotage his father's crops and eventually scared off investors by pretending to be a ghost anytime one of them came to discuss business."

"A living guy who pretended to be a ghost, and now roams the island as one." Logan shakes his head. "The irony."

"That's it." I meet his eyes and a slow smile creeps across my face. The thread of the truth is right there, dangling in front of me. "Whoever is perpetrating the curse and trying to scare off investors is mimicking Yarwen. It says here that there was a tractor accident where the 'ghost' was blamed for the death of a man who sold farm implements and had visited the island to sell some to Yarwen's father. After that, the curse took hold." I flip through several more pages and find another mention of a death. "A laundress slipped and broke her neck while washing his father's clothes. Her coworkers claimed a chill wind swept through the room right before she died."

"And the curse was born," my grandmother says.

Had I felt that very same wind? I continue to scan the rest of the book. It's not very thick, and there is a lot of drama between the lines of dates and facts, but there are no other mentions of the boy, his family, or any curse. There is no author listed for this volume, and it skips around in its timeline. Even the prose seems disjointed, as if there were multiple authors, each with their own voice and perspective.

I pick up the diary, my eyelids heavier yet, and flip through it. I need to stay awake, and probably should get up and do some exercise, rather than reading. I often fall asleep in bed, trying to catch up on my mother's latest pick for the library's book club. Not that the books aren't captivating, I am simply tired and it lulls me to sleep.

The journal is twice as thick as the history book. As I skim it, pieces of Honoree's memories fall out—a ribbon, a pressed flower, a drawing with the words under it in another language. I feel like I'm eavesdropping on her life, but I return to the first page and start reading.

She was fourteen when she began keeping track of events. The usual teenage angst is incorporated in the words detailing her day-to-day activities. Right off the bat, she talks about a boy—but doesn't name him.

My bet is it's Yarwen. He's two years older, and she eagerly joins his quest to respect the island and its inhabitants. Soon, I'm engrossed in the details.

"Anything useful?" Logan asks.

I glance up, realizing everyone is looking at me and that an hour has passed. The storm is over and I no longer feel sleepy. "Useful? No. Fascinating? Most definitely." I move on and realize I'm no longer reading about her crush on the boy or their latest prank on the owners of the estate. "Wait a minute." I scan the next page and the next. "This isn't just a diary."

"What is it then?" my grandmother asks.

I hold it up and show her the page. "This is a recipe, but I don't know for what." Although I have a crawling sensation along my spine at the list of ingredients. "Toad skin? Goat liver?"

The three of them gather around me.

"Not a recipe book nor a diary." Tabitha grins as if I've given her a beloved gift. "That's a grimoire you've got there, Avalon."

EIGHT

My grandmother is correct—what started as a diary of a young girl who grew up on the island turned into the spell book of a witch.

As Logan returns to his chair and Persephone paces, I skip ahead and find more embedded within the descriptions as she gets older. A new boy enters the picture, a man really, twenty-years-old and a seaman.

Tabitha taps the paper. "That's a protection spell."

The pages are filled with them. "To ensure he returned safely from fishing expeditions."

She nods.

There's a mention of a statue he carved from wood while at sea, and a rough drawing of it. She claims the likeness to be the goddess of the waterways and mentions offerings she makes to it where it sits next to her bed.

As I find various entries that snag my interest, I summarize them out loud to the others. "Eventually, they married and had a child. Here's one about a devastating storm that came up out of nowhere. She says it caught everyone, including her grandmother, who was some kind of weather expert, by surprise. Oh…"

"What?" Logan sits forward in his chair.

Apparently, I'm not the only one invested in this girl's story. "Her husband was out at sea when it hit." Quickly, I scan the next couple entries, and then sigh with relief. "She wrote a spell, then went out in the storm to call to the goddess and make an offering on the beach. The fishing boat did not come home, but her husband washed ashore two days later on a plank of wood. He claimed the boat sank and he thought he was a dead man, but swore he felt someone lift him from the turbulent waters and lay him on that piece of floating debris." I glance up. "After that, it sounds like the villagers became fearful of Honoree. Started calling her—"

"Let me guess," my grandmother interrupts. "A witch."

The story has definitely taken a turn I wasn't expecting, considering I thought I would learn more about Yarwen and his family. "Both she and her husband tried to assure everyone that it was the goddess, but odd things began happening around the island."

"And she was blamed for them," Persephone says.

I read on. "In the last entry, she writes, 'They come for my life. I give myself over to the goddess of the seas. May she protect me and those I hold dear.'" Closing the book, my heart gives a tug. "That's it."

Heavy silence hangs in the room. The last of the burning wood crackles, sending up a spark.

"They drowned her." My grandmother shakes her head, staring into the dying embers. "People are idiots."

"There's something bothering me about the time-frame." None of the entries list a year, but I revisit several pages, locating an account about construction of a new and improved marina, which I'd skipped over. I point to the history edition near Logan's elbow. "When did they start offering charter fishing?"

He flips through several sections. "Looks like the late nineteen-sixties. They tried commercial fishing and it flopped, so the owners turned the place into a resort and offered charter fishing to lure in vacationers and adventurists. Called it Hemingway Adventures, after Ernest Hemingway. It took about a decade, but then they landed a deal with a major backer and built a bigger marina, adding six more bays and boats with the latest in technology. A group rented one of the day charters to go diving and found a lost treasure. That made headlines around the world and in the nineties, things were booming. They even built a theatre here and drew in famous actors from all over. Many of the islanders objected, stating all the business was harming the ecosystem and diminishing fish populations which created issues for them to feed their own families."

Honoree wasn't as old as I'd suspected. "Is there any mention about this major storm that came through, or about drowning a witch?"

As he scans the history, I replace the ribbon, pressed flower, and drawing into the journal/grimoire. Had she truly been drowned? What happened to her husband? Her child?

"Nothing about your witch, but there is mention of a devastating hurricane that came through in 1993. Destroyed the marina and all the boats. Says here, half the islanders were washed out to sea, and"—he glances up at me with a stunned expression—"a single man survived when the fishing boat he was in went down in the storm with all its crew."

A chill runs down my spine. "Does it say what his name was?"

"Buku Livingston."

I nearly drop the diary. "Our boat captain?"

"Do you know any other Bukus?"

I rub my temple where a headache is forming. "Honoree is the ghost I saw on the boat."

"You saw a spirit on the ride over? You didn't say anything."

"I ignored her. I didn't want to upset you."

He tosses the book on the table and lifts me from my chair to gather me in his arms. "I should know better than to think there won't be ghosts wherever we go."

"I'm sorry. It's part of who I am. I can't turn it off."

"I know." He kisses me lightly. "I'm sorry if I've put pressure on you to ignore that."

"The pair of ye are the cutest," my grandmother says.

Persephone snorts. "Cute or not, you still have a killer to bring to justice."

She's right. I give Logan a squeeze and step back. "Sid?" I call. "Irma? I need to talk to you."

There's a knock on the library door. We all exchange a look.

"Ghosts don't knock, do they?" Logan asks.

"No." I stride for it. "Murderers don't usually either."

"Sure they do." He stops me and grabs the poker from the set next to the fireplace. "Especially when they're locked out."

He raises the weapon with one hand and prepares to open the door with the other.

Persephone rolls her eyes. "It's not the killer."

"Oh." He lowers the poker and out of the corner of my eye I see Tabitha shrink and morph into her cat self.

We find Wasmee on the other side of the threshold when Logan eases the heavy door open. "Help," she whispers, and then tumbles into my husband's arms.

He catches her, the poker dropping with a clang, and then gently lowers her to the floor. "What's wrong?"

"I can't see." Her lips tremble and her eyes dart around aimlessly. She's no longer wearing her patch. "The curse has come for me. I don't have long to live."

He waves a hand in front of her face, but her eyes don't track it. "How did you make it here if you're blind?"

"Fred," I say, as the goat's stench alerts me to his presence a second before he wanders in. He's still soaked and dripping dirty water.

The psychic grips Logan's shirt sleeve. "I was in my living room. There was a flash and then...nothing. I must have passed out. When I awoke, I was blind."

"Could have been lightning." I'd learned a lot about their strikes several months ago. They could cause a host of odd illnesses and worse.

Tabby's golden eyes search the woman's face. Persephone seems to read her mind. "She would have evidence of it on her body, her clothes, something."

True. Logan sits Wasmee up and we examine her. Not even a strand of hair is singed.

"Do you know anything about Honoree Livingston?" I ask.

The others, including my feline grandmother frown, but what else is there to do? We can't take her to a doctor, and in my opinion, she's lucky to be alive regardless if she got too close to a bolt of lightning *or* the murderer.

"Livingston?" Wasmee tenses, then shakes her head.

"You're lying," I say.

A corner of her lips twitch. Her eyes slide to the side. "I don't know what you're talking about. There is no one by that name here."

"But you've seen her ghost, just like I have."

She shakes her head, sending her earrings flying about. "Why are you asking about her?"

"Curiosity," I lie. "I read some of the island history. She played a role in it."

Her chin comes up but she doesn't glance at me. Tabby closes in on silent paws, her eyes locked on the psychic's face. I swear Wasmee senses she's near and draws back slightly. "I knew an Honoree May."

Knew, as in past tense. Honoree seemed about as rare of a name as Buku. "Was she married to a fisherman?"

A dip of her chin. "She was."

"Was she drowned by the islanders for being a witch?"

Her unseeing eyes lock on a spot near my belly button. Her voice is quiet, as if she's afraid Honoree's ghost might be listening. "That's not in the history books. How do you know about that?"

"I read her diary."

Her body jerks like I've pinched her and her gaze rises. "Her *what*?"

I study her as closely as my grandmother is. "Lots of interesting facts in it."

"Where did you find such a thing?"

"You did know her then?"

Sadness etches her face. "She was a good person, an honest one."

Logan picks up the poker from where he dropped it. "She was your friend?"

"She was more than that." Wasmee struggles to stand and Logan helps her. Tabby shifts to avoid being stepped on. Once the woman is on her feet, she places a hand over her heart and tears line her eyes. "Honoree was my mother."

NINE

"Now we're getting somewhere," Persephone says. She gives me a go ahead motion.

That's angel speak for "you're on the right track. Keep going."

"Let me get this straight." I stare into Wasmee's eyes, but she does indeed seem blind. "You're the daughter of the witch the islanders sent to a watery grave, but you're trying to run us off with all this talk about a curse."

Her lips firm.

"Your dad is Buku, our captain."

Her jaw clenches. Still, she says nothing.

I continue. "You don't seem the least bit scared of the murderer, and I'm guessing your father has a vendetta against those who drowned your mother."

"No one killed her." Wasmee is defiant. "She took her own life."

That heavy silence from earlier returns. The lingering heat from the fire disappears and a chill sweeps over my shoulders. Like before, it's as if a spirit has brushed past.

"Why would she do that?" Logan asks solemnly.

The last of the flames wink out and we are plunged into total darkness. Fred brays, rattling the windows and I throw my hands over my ears. "Stop that!"

The awful sound ceases and we all breathe a sigh of relief.

"The goat is only protecting me," Wasmee insists. "He hates it when I get upset."

Logan inclines his head at the animal. "Like that atrocious noise doesn't upset you?"

"He's my familiar." Her hands are barely visible in the gloom when she holds them out. "Can I have my mother's diary? Please?"

I place it in her outstretched palms, feeling bad for pushing her so hard. "I'm sorry about what happened. How old were you?"

"Six." She brings the journal to her chest and hugs it. As my eyes adjust to the dark, I notice her cheeks are wet with tears. "That day changed everything. People looked at me as if I had a disease. Kids threatened me. I had no friends, save this goat."

His odor is making my own eyes water, but I cut him some slack, seeing as how he's still with her. "But that would make him pretty old for a goat."

"He's magical." Her voice is reproachful, as if I'm too dense to understand such a thing. "Sounds impossible to those like you who do not understand the invisible world, but—"

"I see ghosts, remember?"

Properly chastised, she nods. "The other voice I hear— one of yours from the spirit world?"

"Yes and no. Persephone is my guardian angel-slash-spirit guide. Also known as a pain in my a—"

The being in question clears her throat loudly. "Nice to meet you."

"The other entity with us is my many-times great grandmother, Tabitha. She's even older than your goat and shapeshifts into a cat."

Wasmee's heavily made up eyes widen. "How....unusual."

"There's nothing you can say that will shock us," I state. I'm *pretty* sure that's true. "Why don't you tell us who the real killer is, and why you've been covering for him?"

A small sob escapes her lips. She seems ready to confess when a large shadow fills the doorway. A fishy odor permeates the already stinky air. "Was, we must go," a heavily accented man says. Our captain. Thunder rumbles in the distance and I wonder if we're in for another storm. "Now!"

She turns toward his sharp voice, as do the rest of us. "But...we can't leave them. You know what will happen."

"No one's leaving anybody." Logan tightens his hold on the iron poker and grabs my elbow. "We're getting off the island with you."

"No," the man argues, blocking our escape. "Only Wasmee."

Logan points the sharp end of the now-weapon at him. "Did you kill the staff?"

Wasmee sucks in a breath. "He wouldn't hurt a fly." She places a hand on the man's chest. "We must help them," she insists.

His jowls shake. "The boat cannot handle so much weight!"

From the depths of the mansion comes a loud bang—the rear door.

"The killer is coming," Buku says in a hushed voice. He waves an arm, rushing us out. "Hurry."

Even Fred wants to leave, his head finding my backside again in the line we form to exit. "Hey," I smack his hat. "Don't be rude."

Tabby races past Wasmee as she crosses the threshold, Buku holding her arm. Footsteps echo in the hall. "Run!" Buku yells.

We do.

The floor is slippery from Fred dripping all over it and my feet go out from under me when I hit a puddle. Logan lifts me as the others rush out. "Are you okay?"

The squeak of shoes on the wooden floors draws closer. In the dark, I can't see the approaching figure, but I feel his presence. "Fine. Go!"

We're nearly to the door when a deep, dramatic voice calls, "You can't escape the curse! They will find you!"

Logan, who jogs daily and is in great shape, shoves me out to the veranda and down the wet steps, nearly carrying me in his haste. The night air is so heavy with humidity, it's hard to breathe. The second storm is indeed threatening, lightning dancing on the water far in the distance.

As I try not to twist my ankle, I lean on Logan for support and make it to the bottom. That voice pings around in my brain and I pull up short, nearly tripping him. The others have run ahead, disappearing down the path. "Wait a minute." I glance at the mansion. There's no one pursuing us. In fact, the doors have been closed. "I know that voice."

As I march back to the house, Logan grabs me by the elbow. "Ava, what the heck are you doing? You can't go in there."

"There's something fishy about all of this, and it's not because we're on an island."

I disengage from his grip and walk up the stairs. He pursues me and stops me before I reach the handles of the double doors.

He grabs my arms and makes me face him. "There's a killer in there. We need to leave and send law enforcement to handle this."

I don't disagree, but something is nagging at me. "I need to talk to the ghosts."

Persephone appears. "She's right. She does."

Tabby bounds up the crumbling steps and meows.

Logan sighs and briefly shuts his eyes before pinning me with a glare. "I can see I'm outvoted, but you realize how dangerous this is."

As if the heaven's agree, thunder booms. I squeeze his hand. "I know it's a lot for you to go along with this. I wish I was normal, believe me, and that I lived and worked in Thornhollow with none of these ghostly issues, but I'm not, and I don't. I feel a responsibility to these spirits. They're stuck here, and everyone has deserted them."

"Not *exactly* true." Persephone angles herself toward the window where I'd noticed movement earlier that day. "But close enough."

"What do you mean?" I ask.

She makes a motion of locking her lips and I roll my

eyes. Tabby claws at the double doors, and Logan glances at her, then to me. "Fine, but let me go first, okay?"

He doesn't wait for my answer and Tabby moves aside. The hinges creak as I place my hand on his back and we return to the foyer.

Whoever was chasing us has disappeared. "If that was the killer, why didn't he pursue us to the beach?" Logan asks quietly.

"Because he wanted to scare us, not murder us." I glance around, but there's little visible in the gloom. "Sid? Irma? Bernie? What game are you guys playing? I need to talk to you. Now."

Irma flickers into view. "Help us," she whispers, then disappears.

"Not useful," I call.

Logan scans the dark entrance. "What happened?"

"Irma popped in," I tell him. "She whispered, 'help us' then vamoosed."

"What does that mean? What should we do?"

With ghosts, it's hard to tell. "I can't cross them over unless they talk to me." It's really all I can do for them, along with seeing that their deaths are avenged. "And it's time for them to move onto the afterlife. I was hoping to get a few questions answered first, though."

Persephone has floated up to the second floor and slides down the curved railing. "Whee!"

"Oh, for heaven's sake," I mutter. "Can you be serious for a moment?"

"Ava? Logan?" Wasmee rushes in, Buku on her heels. "What are you doing? You have to leave!"

"I have to help the...wait. You can see again?"

She freezes, her face that of the cat caught with the

canary in its mouth. "I, well... Yes, it happened at the beach. All of sudden, my sight came back." Her hands motion us toward the exit. "Come, we go now!"

"Hurry," her father insists. "I will not wait any longer. You don't want to be stuck here with a killer, do you?"

Logan crosses his arms. "You're not going anywhere without us." He inclines his head to me. "And she has work to do."

I call again to the ghosts, and when they refuse to appear, Logan, Persephone, Tabby, and I begin a search.

My husband leads the charge as we go from room to room. Not one spirit makes an appearance, but as we enter an upstairs bedroom suite, a man jumps out of a closet and knocks me down.

He sprints for the stairs and Logan tackles him before he gets out the door. I jump up and yell for Logan to be careful as the man fights and squirms like a child hopped on Halloween candy.

Logan, who's taller and outweighs him by thirty pounds, eventually subdues the man enough to get him into a chair by the window. The man is thin and his hair is uncombed. I can't tell his age but he's younger than us.

He fidgets and tries to break free from Logan's hold, then cries out as he peers toward the door. "Wassie! Help!"

Wasmee stands there, swaying on her feet. A flash of lightning shows her face is strained, more tears slipping from her eyes. "Oh, Hart. I tried. I really did."

He speaks in gibberish and neither Logan nor I understand. Persephone translates. "He's made up his own language."

"Why?" I ask as Hartwell wiggles and twitches.

"He's a bit…different." She taps her temple. "Lives up here more than the real world."

Seems too frail to be our killer, but I've learned never to underestimate anybody. "Who is he?"

"No one. Just a boy. He didn't hurt them."

"Then who did?" Logan demands. "Tell us the truth or Ava and I take him to the mainland and turn him over to the authorities."

"No." She rushes in and places a hand on Hart's shoulder. He instantly calms. "It's my fault. All of it. He inherited the gift from me, but it drove him mad."

Things click into place. I gawk. "He's your *son*? And he sees ghosts?" That could definitely cause you to lose your marbles.

She gives a solemn nod. "I tried to help him, but…"

"Didn't meant to scare you," the kid says, his gaze flicking to me and away. "Wanted you to leave."

Sid pops in. "He's telling the truth. He was trying to protect you. It's dangerous here and it was his idea that we frighten you enough that you left and told the new owner the place is cursed."

"It was your voice I heard acting the part of the killer, but it was Hart's footsteps, wasn't it?"

Sid nods. "We weren't expecting guests, that's the truth, and once you showed up, Hart insisted we chase you off."

"And keep anyone else from coming," Wasmee adds. "We thought the legend of the curse might keep everyone away."

Logan sighs and releases his hold when Hart grips onto Wasmee's arm and begins weeping softly. "He needs a professional."

"No!" The young man shakes his head violently. "No leave."

Wasmee strokes his hair, making soothing sounds. "I can't take him from the island. He can't handle the stress of the real world."

My heart sinks. "But why did he kill the staff? Did they threaten to take him from you?"

"He didn't." She lifts her head and straightens her spine, indignant. "I swear."

Logan pinches the bridge of his nose. "And we're back where we started. Then who did?"

The temperature in the room plummets and the earlier chill wind rushes over me once more, raising goose flesh on my bare skin. A soft whistling begins.

Wasmee gasps. The boy presses himself back into the chair, eyes bulging as he stares at the room behind me. Tabby meows, a high-pitched sound that could give Fred a run for his money in the caterwauling department. A sinking dread in my belly, I swallow hard.

Sensing the answer to his question is now present, Logan scans the room. "You've got to be kidding."

Hart points with a trembling finger. "Them! They hurt Miss Irma and the others."

The whistling stops. Teeth beginning to chatter, I let loose a slow breath and turn my head to look over my shoulder.

Dozens of ghosts are lined up behind me, each with murder in their eyes.

TEN

"This should be fun," Persephone says.

Sid makes a squeak and disappears.

Swiveling, I back toward Logan. "Not fun. Not good."

"It's the islanders," Wasmee whispers in my ear. She touches my shoulder, as if in camaraderie. "They have built up enough energy between them that they can do things now. Not like normal ghosts—they're much, much stronger. Their leader has so much hate in her heart, she is particularly powerful."

Logan steps in front of me, not knowing exactly what's going on, but ready to defend and protect anyway. I love this man.

"I need to do a mass crossing," I announce. "But we may need that poker first."

It lies on the bed where he dropped it when he pursued Hart.

Buku scurries in to join us. "They will kill you. We

tried to protect the others, scare them all away, but none of you will leave us be. You just keep coming."

Boy, do I wish Mama was here. She's always good at thinking on her feet in front of large crowds. Her and Winter. I could use both of them. Winter could help me with the crossing of these poor souls.

I clear my throat, trying to channel each of those dynamic women, my mentors in so many ways.

I shift out from behind Logan, patting his hand to let him know it's all right. I'm lucky to have him, as well as Mama and Winter, in my life. "The island is beautiful and I know how incredibly special it is to you since it's your home."

The central ghost, a woman with a head wrap similar to Wasmee's, steps forward, towering over me. This must be the leader. She crosses her arms and peers down a long, flared nose at me. Her words are heavily accented. "You know nothing." She spits on the ground.

I hold steady, refusing to back up so much as an inch. "I grew up in a small town. Not an island, but, when I was younger, it felt like one. It's a place where we all know every-one, you can't get away from the gossip, yet you also have plenty of friends and family who are always there for you. When I was a teen, I couldn't wait to bail, get away from all the nosy busybodies. I went to college, got a job, thought I was happy. When my aunt died last year, I returned home to handle her estate. I ended up staying, because of those very same reasons. I *love* my hometown and all its people. I'm sure that's why you're trying to protect your island."

My words don't seem to sway her. "This place belongs to us,"—she jabs her chest with a thumb—"and always has.

You are not welcome, and you will pay, like the others, for disrespecting it."

"The staff were your descendants. Why would you kill them?"

She grimaces. "Traitors, they are. They should have kept our ways, not allowed the constant stream of mainlanders to come and destroy our island. We've had enough!"

Hart begins speaking his gibberish again, rocking in the chair. Wasmee tries to comfort him. Logan brushes his fingers across mine. "Do I need to get that poker?"

"Not just yet." I put my hands on my hips and do my best imitation of Mama. "You've been disregarded and treated poorly, and I'm sorry about that, but tormenting this poor boy and murdering the others does not correct the injustices done to you. If you want a solution, then we have to figure it out together. There's no going back and fixing things—we can only move forward."

The group of ghosts behind her grumble and shuffle their incorporeal feet. "Get off our island," the leader sneers.

"No." I stand my ground. "Either you work with me to honor your ancestors and culture, or I'll send you to the great beyond and figure it out myself."

I'm not sure she's ever had anyone stand up to her, and she must see some of the Dixie Fantome temper in my stance. My mother didn't get to be mayor of Thornhollow by being a pushover.

"You are not sending us anywhere," the woman declares.

Time to channel more Winter. I smile, as if I have a secret that challenges that statement. I sort of do. In my head, I call on the white light door that aids me when crossing over ghosts. It's the bridge to the afterlife. As it forms, I notice several in the crowd glancing at a version they too now see.

Quiet gasps and murmurs flow through the mob. Most of them float back a step or two. Even Wasmee sucks in a sharp breath. She's able to see it as well.

"So... pretty," Hart says. I sense him stand. He and his mother step to my other side, the four of us forming a wall.

Tabby nears my feet and yowls at the ghostly woman. Persephone sidles up to Logan's other side. Together, we are as formidable as the spectrals in the room.

"There's peace on the other side of that light," I tell them. "Your family and friends are there waiting for you. You can't change the past, but you can affect the future of this island. I have several ideas to educate visitors, as well as celebrate and pay tribute to you and your ancestors. This is a wonderful place for a cultural learning center. Let me help you."

Two of them float toward the light. As soon as they are near it, even though others try to tug them away, they disappear.

"No," their leader cries. She places herself between it and the rest of the group. "She lies! We must stay here to protect the island!"

"We can have it declared a nature preserve," Logan says, picking up on my thoughts. "I happen to be friends with the new owner." He glances at me, as if to suggest that once we explain to Judge Barlow what has happened, he and Logan may no longer be friends. We'll have to tackle that when we get home. "I'll do everything possible to make sure he does right by you."

Honoree appears, gliding toward the light and oohing

over it. Her presence forces the leader of the vengeful spirits aside. "Is that heaven?"

Close enough. I've been in that light a couple times, but never finished the journey. I have Logan to thank for keeping me here. Still, it's easier for me to convince earthbound spirits to go into it since I've experienced what it's like. "I've had two near-death events, and I can tell you, it's total bliss."

"I miss my family," a male ghost says, staring into it. "Are they really there? On the other side?"

"Yes," Hart says out of the blue. I'd nearly forgotten he was right next to me. "I can sense them. Can't you?"

His face is euphoric. Wasmee beams with pride. "Such a unique child," she whispers to me. "Closer to that side of the veil than this one."

I don't envy him. It's not easy being a sensitive like he is. "Hart's right. They are indeed."

The man fades into it and Honoree claps. "Who's next?"

"Don't go," Buku pleads to her. "I need you."

"She can visit any time she wishes." I glance at Persephone to be sure this is the case. Most souls can check on loved ones in the physical plane. She nods and I'm grateful for her presence in this moment. "Honoree can return as a spirit guide for you."

Two more go into the light. The leader grows more and more agitated, attempting to stop them, but she can't. Her power is dimming as they take theirs from her.

Wetness coats Buku's cheeks. "You'll be with me every day like you are now?"

Honoree kisses his lips, her own barely grazing his. He probably can't even feel them, they are so feathery light.

Wasmee is crying, too. "We love you, Mama, and wish you could be with us always, but you need to cross over. Come back when you can."

"I'll always be in your hearts," she says, kissing her daughter and grandson as well. Hart's eyes gleam with joy. "And you know you can't get rid of me this easily." She offers a cheeky grin. "You bet your turnips I'll be back to watch over each of you for the rest of your days."

She is no longer dripping water. Her clothes and hair are dry. Appearing younger than I had originally guessed, she gives a wave and floats backward until her form disappears in a burst of light.

"My love." Buku reaches for her, but she is gone. Wasmee goes to him, taking his outstretched hand. He folds into her, weeping softly. Logan and I watch the comfort she offers her father, and Hart joins in, wrapping his thin arms around them.

"You," the leader of the spirits snarls. "I will kill you."

I duck when she swoops at me, but I'm late and her body slams into mine. She's still got enough punch that I go down like I've been hit by a linebacker.

My temple cracks on the arm of the chair and pain blooms. I tumble sideways as Logan yells, "Ava!"

ELEVEN

lood trickles into my eyes and I lift a hand to ward off her next attack, but she doesn't make contact this time. In a daring leap, Logan snatches up the poker and swings.

Smack! The vengeful ghost goes flying across the room.

Right, in fact, into the doorway of light.

She lets out a shocked gasp, then vanishes.

While I prefer to get consent when I send earthbound spirits into the light, sometimes that's not an option. "Nice shot," I say as Wasmee rushes to my side. "And you couldn't even see her."

Logan is already beside me, helping me to my feet. "Did I get her?"

"Home run," I tell him, trying not to sway.

Hart leads Buku to the chair and makes him sit. The older man puts his head in his hands.

"Did you mean what you said?" Wasmee asks. "About turning the island into a refuge and visitor learning center?"

Logan examines my bleeding temple. "Yes, but we have to figure out what to do with those dead bodies downstairs. Nothing will happen until their murders are investigated and those will be hard to explain since ghosts are the perpetrators."

Sid pops in. "Bury us in the old cemetery," he suggests. "No one has to know it was murder. None of us has any living family, so there's nobody will ask after us. We're part of the island legend now."

Irma floats through the wall nodding vigorously. "Wasmee and Hart can take over. They can run the visitor center and teach people about us. About our heritage. Buku knows this land, and the waters surrounding it, like the back of his hand. He can teach conservation and share the old ways with those who want to know about them."

Bernie is next to join in. "And my recipes. They're a part of our history, too. They've been handed down from generation to generation—I got all of them from my grandmother, who got them from her mother, and so forth. Turn them into a cookbook and sell them to support the upkeep of the center. They're worth a fortune, I tell ya."

I nod, thinking that over. "That's a fantastic idea. Are you all going to cross or are you staying?"

"I'm staying." Rommy, in his coveralls, slinks in. The others nod in agreement. "My body's by the big palm tree. Will you bury me, too?"

Logan uses his handkerchief to clean the blood from my cheek. I repeat what Rommy has said. "And where is that particular tree?" Logan asks. "The island is full of palms."

"It's in the very center," Hart tells us. "The first family to make this place home all those centuries ago marked it as a ceremonial tree. Every year, it is recognized as the island's guardian. None of the hurricanes have knocked it down or harmed it. It's protected. I can show you where it is."

"We'll handle the burials," Buku says. "It's only right that we do it."

"I was making an offering," Rommy explains, "and the ghosts came out of nowhere and knocked my head into the trunk. It was lights out for me."

I rub my skull. A dull throb has replaced the sting of the cut. "I'm sorry about all of you ending up at their will."

"Is there retribution on the other side?" Buku asks. "They should be punished."

I don't really know about that, but I do know from Persephone there is karma. "I let the Big Guy work all that out, but I believe they now understand how wrong it was to take their anger out on all of you. I bet they're sorry."

Honoree appears in a *pop*, a bubble of sunshine. "They do! I just saw all of them and they *know* now." The way she stresses the word makes its meaning clear to all of us. Winter always says that those who have crossed know everything. They are tapped in and turned on to Source, the ultimate internet, so to speak. "They said to tell you how very sorry they are. They're coming back as spirit guides for you...if you want."

Buku jets out of the chair and tries to hug her. His arms go right through her ethereal body, and she giggles and motions for him to be still. He smiles gleefully at her and she gently touches his face.

He can feel it this time. It takes a lot of energy, but she, too, is "tapped in." Like Persephone, she can do more than most ghosts—she can appear almost corporeal and even make things move.

Logan and I say goodbye to the ghostly staff and leave the family to their reunion. Morning is approaching, and the second storm has blown out to sea, revealing a lavender colored horizon.

Logan makes a cold pack out of the last of the ice in the freezer and guides me to a chair on the veranda. Fred ambles out to stand too close but I don't chase him away. Persephone and Tabby join us.

I can see my husband is at odds with himself as he paces and scratches his chin. I rest my head on the back of the wooden chair. My sundress is dirty, my sandals ruined. "What do you think about not reporting the staff deaths?"

He stops and leans a hip on the railing. When it wobbles, he seems to think better of it and stands near me, hands on his hips. "We'd be negligent in doing so, but the alternative would create a lot of significant problems for Hart and his family."

"They did help save our lives," I point out, "I feel like we owe them the courtesy. If anyone asks, they can report that Sid and the others simply took off after the hurricane. If we report the murders, the place will never be successful as a nature preserve or anything else. Hart could end up in prison or a mental hospital, even though he had nothing to do with the crimes. The island would become a documentary on some cable channel or podcast. Definitely not what I want."

"I know." He stares at the approaching sunrise. "I'd like Wasmee's family to have some peace, just like those ghosts, but it goes against my principles to cover up murder."

I stand and hug him from behind. "Me, too, but in this

case, we know who the culprits are, and trust me, they've been brought to justice by a higher power."

His shoulders relax a bit. "You're right." He turns in my arms and frowns at my injury. "You're getting quite a lump. We need to get you to the mainland and have you checked for a concussion."

"You're not concussed," Persephone tells me. "But you do need to get home."

Her tone is foreboding and I see trepidation in her face.

I repeat the part about my health to Logan, then ask her, "Are Mama and Daddy okay?"

She waves me off and starts to float away as the horizon grows a warm pink. "Your parents are fine. It's Kit you need to worry about."

Kit works as a private detective and recently moved to Thornhollow. She sees spirits, too, and has claimed to see the future as well, although I have my doubts. Her intuitive skills do make her a fairly accurate guesser. "What's wrong with her? Is it a ghost problem?"

Persephone glances over her shoulder. "Isn't it always?"

Before I can question her further, she disappears. Logan takes my hand and pulls me close. "Who's in trouble now?"

"Kit, and apparently it involves a spirit."

He kisses my forehead. "As you keep reminding me, ghost whispering is part of your job. It's who you are."

I pinch his waist and he laughs, flinching away. "It is," I concede, "but I sure wish I could have a day off."

Persephone's voice floats past me, a hint of teasing in it. "No rest for the wicked."

I ignore her as Logan says, "I'll go get our captain."

As he leaves, Tabby stands on the top step, eyeing the goat. The beast chews his piece of straw that never seems to be consumed.

"Can you read his mind?" I ask jokingly. Since Persephone left without her, I assume she's going back with Logan and I. "Wasmee claims she can understand him."

The cat morphs into my grandmother, naked as a jaybird. She leans over to look Fred in the eyes. "He's no dumb beast, that's for sure, are ye, Yarwen?"

She winks at him and the goat's mouth falls open, the straw dropping to the porch.

"Wait," I say. "*That's* Yarwen?"

"Ye magic is different than mine, yet similar. Why a goat?"

But Yarwen simply stares, mouth agape. Something changes in his eyes, though.

"Ah, I see," my grandmother says. There's commotion inside the house and I fear our new friends are about to get an eyeful. "Twas not you're doing, now was it?" She shakes a chastising finger at him. "That's what you get for breaking the heart of a witch!"

"Tabitha," I warn as the others draw near. The door begins to open. "Cat. Now."

Just as Logan, Wasmee, Hart, and Buku spill out onto the porch, she shifts, but not before they get a brief flash of her nude form.

As Tabby the cat once more, she sits and cleans her paws, glancing up at them with her golden eyes and meows lazily.

"Was that...?" Wasmee gives me an incredulous glance. I nod and she blinks. "That's serious magic."

I pet my grandmother's furry head. "It's something, all right."

Three hours later, Logan and I park in front of the house and drag ourselves inside. Rosie and Jen, my employees, are shocked to see us. I beg off from answering their questions and we collapse into bed and sleep for hours.

When I wake, I feel refreshed, and snuggle next to Logan. He draws me to him and I lay my head on his shoulder. "I'm sorry," he says. "I promise to make it up to you after our official wedding in October."

"Don't worry about it." I pat his chest. "I'm actually happy that we were able to help all of those people, both the living and the dead. I *am* having second thoughts about that cruise we signed up for."

He rubs his eyes. "I'll cancel the reservations. It was bad enough on an island, I can't imagine being on a ship in the middle of the ocean with a bunch of ghosts."

I'm relieved he sees my conundrum. "I was thinking maybe we could stay at the Nottingham. At least I've already dealt with its resident spirit and crossed her over."

He's quiet for a moment, considering it. "You don't think there's more?"

There are always more. "It's possible, but at least it's close to home." I raise up on my elbow. "And honestly, there's no place I'd rather be than right here with you and the people we love."

Tabby meows and I realize we have an audience. "Pets, too," I add.

Moxley, Logan's basset hound, barks from his bed on the floor, adding his agreement.

Logan smiles. "Have I told you lately how brilliant you are?"

"I can never hear that statement too many times."

"I'll book a suite today. Since they love you, maybe we'll get the entire third floor."

"Good." I snuggle down once again. "Then we better get started on those promises we made to Wasmee and her family."

He sighs. "And you have to check in with Kit."

"And we have a wedding to plan."

He squeezes me tight and kisses the top of my forehead. "Life with you is always an adventure."

That it was.

DON'T MISS *Ava's next adventure in Wedding Bells and Psychic Spells, coming later this year! She and Logan have their hands full preparing for their second set of nuptials and saving Kit from an untimely death!*

Don't miss the next exciting adventure! Sign up for Nyx's Cozy Clues Mystery Newsletter.

And check out these magical stories:

Sister Witches Of Raven Falls Mystery Series

Sister Witches of Raven Falls Special Collection
Of Potions and Portents
Of Curses and Charms
Of Stars and Spells
Of Spirits and Superstition

Confessions of a Closet Medium Cozy Mystery Series

Confessions of a Closet Medium Special Collection
Pumpkins & Poltergeists

Magic & Mistletoe
Hearts & Haunts
Vows & Vengeance
Cupcakes & Corpses
Tea Leaves & Troubled Spirits
Haunted Honeymoon

Sister Witches of Story Cove Cozy Mystery Series

Cinder
Belle
Snow
Ruby
Zelle

Candy Shop Witch Paranormal Cozy Mystery Series (Coming 2023)

Tricks and Treats (including bonus prequel)
Candy and Creeps
Gum and Ghouls
Sweets and Spirits
Sugar and Shudder
Bonbons and Bones

ABOUT THE AUTHOR

USA Today Bestselling Author Nyx Halliwell grew up on TV shows like *Buffy the Vampire Slayer* and *Charmed,* and loves writing stories as much as she loves baking and crafting. She believes in magick and that we each carry it inside us.

Connect with Nyx today and see pictures of her pets, be the first to know about new books and sales! Receive a FREE copy of the Whitethorne Book of Spells and Recipes and a coupon code for a free download of her Magical Adventures Set by signing up for her newsletter http://eepurl.com/gwKHB9

CONNECT WITH NYX TODAY!

FREE ebook with newsletter signup!!

Website: nyxhalliwell.com

Email: nyxhalliwellauthor@gmail.com
Bookbub https://www.bookbub.com/profile/nyx-halliwell
Amazon amazon.com/author/nyxhalliwell

Facebook: https://www.facebook.com/
NyxHalliwellAuthor/

Sign up for Nyx's Cozy Clues Mystery Newsletter and be the FIRST to learn about new releases, sales, behind-the-scenes trivia about the book characters, and pictures of Nyx's pets!

DEAR MAGICAL READER

I hope you enjoyed this story! If you did, and would be so kind, would you leave a review on Goodreads, Bookbub, or your favorite book retailer? I would REALLY appreciate it!

A review lets hundreds, if not thousands, of potential readers know what you enjoyed about the book, and helps them make wise buying choices. It's the best word-of-mouth around.

The review doesn't have to be anything long! Pretend you're sharing the story with a good friend. Pick out one or more characters, scenes, or dialogue that made you smile, laugh, or warmed your heart, and tell them about it. Just a few sentences is perfect!

Thank you for supporting my dream, as well as my small business.

Blessed be,

Nyx 🤍